Buy The Horse A Guinness

And Other Wee Tales of Ireland

Written by

David K. McDonnell

Illustrated by
Rob Wilkinson

ISBN10: 09860385-1-2 ISBN13: 978-0-9860385-1-8

Names: McDonnell, David K. | Wilkinson, Robert, illustrator
Title: Buy The Horse A Guinness, And Other Wee Tales of Ireland / by David K. McDonnell; illustrations by Robert Wilkinson
Description: First edition, 2017
Summary: A collection of eight short stories
Story Titles: Buy the Horse a Guinness – Irish Zombies – The Apprentice & the Baker – The Connemara Fisherman – Lochlann the Leprechaun – The Spaewife and the Barnacle Geese – The Wiser Adviser to the King – The Annual Killing of a Barber
Subjects 1. Tales – Ireland. 2. Folklore – Ireland. 3. Short Stories -- Fiction

Printed in the United States, United Kingdom, European Union and Australia.

Published by
Burrowing Owl Press
Grand Traverse Bay, Kewadin, Michigan U.S.A.
www.clandonnell.net
clandonnell@gmail.com

Introduction

I am an Irish storyteller – a seanchaí in the words of the Irish. I've told tales at Irish and Celtic festivals, Irish pubs, bookstores, libraries, and any other forum which would have me. I've performed throughout the United States and in Ireland. Perhaps I'll expand into more countries soon.

The larger Irish clans had their own seanchaí who were called out for feasts and festivals. Often times, a seanchaí was a vagabond, traveling storyteller. He treked from village to village telling stories – often for no more than food and shelter. I've been paid a few bucks for my storytelling -- barely enough to cover the costs of travel -- and provided a hotel room and some food. I am, indeed, a throw-back to the seanchaí of ancient Ireland.

Many folk have asked if I had a written collection of stories. Until now, I had to answer "No". My stories were in my head, and I've lost track of how many are buried in there. I kept some notes to refresh my recollection and to avoid missing entire sections of a story. But I hadn't previously written any of them down.

Writing these stories turned into a major challenge. I never told any of these the same way twice. I enjoy reacting to a vocal audience and taking the stories in different directions, depending upon the reaction and input of the crowd. For this book, I had to decide which version might read better on a written page, and made some significant changes to make each story an entertaining read. And I picked out eight of my favorites.

These are all originally oral stories – created to be told, not read. There is something about live storytelling which is inherently different from writing. A different energy is involved. Hand gestures, eye contact, tone of voice, dialect, pacing and pausing, all influence audience reaction to and understanding of an oral story. The audience cannot go back to re-read a prior page or paragraph, and the storyteller and the listener are constantly propelled forward. There is no rewind button. Perhaps this is why I've fallen in love with oral storytelling.

I added a postcript to each story, in case you're interested in the source of the story and how it evolved.

I also added a pronunciation guide within each story to assist readers. Irish words can be baffling to English speakers (and Scottish Gaelic even more baffling). Don't feel bad if you mispronounce any words. There are dozens of dialects within the small island of Ireland and many, many Irish words are pronounced multiple ways. My favorite example is the pronunciation of Ireland's largest city – it's often DUB-lin, almost as often DOO-blin, and sometimes with three syllables as DUB-ba-lin. Seanchaí, by the way, is pronounced SHAN-ah-key.

As the Irish might say, bain sult as (usually pronounced BAHN-suhl-tahs). The literal translation is "take pleasure in", but the Irish use the phrase as the English would use the word "enjoy".

I indeed hope you enjoy these stories and the wonderful world of Irish storytelling from an American seanchaí.

Special thanks to:

Gavin Grieves at gav@grievesdesign.com for the cover design

Colin McDonnell for his brilliant editing and comedic talents

Courtney and Scott Marlowe for their overall assistance and support

My publisher, Linda McDonnell's Burrowing Owl Press.
She agreed to publish this book in exchange for my making her coffee
every morning.

Everyone who has heard my stories and encouraged me to continue on –
with both oral storytelling and publication of this book

I dedicate this book to my children:

Kirsten Kelly,
Courtney Erin,
Kyle Patrick, and
Colin David.

I loved telling them stories when they were wee ones.
I'm terribly proud of the way they've grown into adults.
I do not know if there is any correlation.

Contents

Irish Zombies

The Samhain festival begins tonight and Ciara was enchanted. It would be, as always, the biggest festival of the year. The musicians will play their instruments, the singers will sing, the dancers will dance, and the storytellers will captivate the clan with tales of glory and wonder.

This is the time when young men in the village aggressively court young women, while the village men act especially frisky with their wives.

Ciara noticed last year that a number of babies were born in the village during the summer, which she reckoned to be about nine months after the festival. She wondered whether any of the boys in the festival would court her, although at her age she was not terribly interested.

Autumn is the busiest time of year, and Ciara was glad it was finally over. For two months, her family cut turf from a nearby field and stacked it high next to their house. Cutting turf was difficult work, as was carrying it to the house. But it would be cold soon and they had enough grass and organic soil to burn all winter. Father would start a fire in a week or so and keep it going until spring.

The cattle and sheep raised by the villagers roamed the countryside since spring. Ciara's brothers and other young men from the village rounded them up a fortnight ago and brought

Ciara *Kee-AR-ah*
Samhain *SAH-win* or *SOW-in*
Poitín *POE-tin* or *POE-teen*

them close to home. The herd would stay fenced within the village pale for the winter.

Everyone in the village participated in the harvest. Last spring came late but the fall was long and warm. The crops had plenty of time to ripen. Everything has been harvested and put away for winter storage. Ciara helped dry the grains in kilns, while others stored food in barrels and clay pots. Some were sealed in pits to keep fresh through the winter. Some of the grains were fermented and distilled for the poitín. The men loved the poitín, although they would get quite silly if they drank too much.

All of this was hard work! Now that the work was done, it was time for the festival.

Ciara's brothers spent the day gathering wood and setting up huge piles for the bonfires. The boys set up a pile in the center of the village and others along the path leading out. They planned to light the fires as soon as the sun set tonight.

Ciara helped her mother make a stew. Father butchered a lamb yesterday and today some of it boiled in a large pot. Mother added some greens, onions, and turnips while Ciara stirred the pot. It smelled delicious and it was indeed a meal fit for a noble. Other villagers did much the same and a rich aroma filled the entire community.

But the bonfires were not being set for the people in the village. Nor would the villagers enjoy the scrumptious meals being prepared. In fact, no living person would, as the bonfires and meals were not for the living at all.

They were for the dead!

Ciara believed, as did all Celts, that a person who died during the year remained in some sort of dormant state. Even while the body decayed, the spirit remained alive until the end of the year. On Samhain, the dead began the journey to the otherworld.

This was a well-known fact at the time, although it was not known where this otherworld was. Storytellers told tales of the otherworld, but these stories were not all the same.

Some tellers regaled long journeys to a world way above the earth, where the dead lived among the clouds and stars. Others told dark tales of the otherworld way below the earth, with hidden caves and tunnels only the dead could see.

Others told stories of the dead who stayed neither above nor below the earth. They moved to a place on the surface of the earth so horrifying that no living person ever wished to go there. They spent eternity at this place only fit for dead people.

The Celts called this place – Ohio!

The villagers wanted the dead to find their way, wherever it was they were going. This was, perhaps, out of the respect for the dead. But truth be told, the living did not want the dead to stay around too long in the village. It was best to help them move on to the otherworld.

Everyone was pretty sure that the dead could not see very well. This was obvious with any examination of a dead person. Usually, the eyes were closed, and if dead for any length of time, their eyes are not even there! It would be a wonder if a dead person could see at all.

So to help out the sightless dead, the villagers built the huge bonfires on the paths leading outside of the village. Even the blind could follow the light, everyone thought, and find their way to the otherworld.

There was another fact of which the villagers felt fairly certain. And that is, the dead are hungry! This was also plain to see with any examination of the dead. Within a short time of death, the dead withered away to nothing but skin and bones. It wasn't terribly long before the dead were nothing but bones. It was quite obvious – a dead person had not had a decent meal since the day they died.

So everyone knew that the dead must be fed. They must have the strength to make it to the otherworld, wherever that was. That is why Ciara and her mother made the pot of stew – so that the dead could feast upon it before they were on their way.

Mother offered to set a place at the table in the house for the dead. Ciara would have nothing of it. She thought it too strange to have a dead person sitting across the table.

Ciara was particularly distressed at the thought of dinner with Aunt Mary. Mary was by far her favorite aunt. She was a large woman and often smothered Ciara deep into her breasts with her hugs. Ciara loved having Aunt Mary over to the house for any occasion. But that was when she was alive. Mary died of a mysterious ailment earlier in the summer. It would be more than a wee bit eerie to have her skeletal remains sitting across the supper table now on Samhain.

Ciara was also a bit nervous about her neighbor, Seamus. He was a young warrior who died in a battle last spring. In fact, Seamus lost his head. An enemy warrior swung his two-handed sword across Seamus' neck, and severed the head from the rest of the body. After the battle, the villagers buried Seamus' body. They never did find his head.

.   Ciara liked Seamus. He was a friendly enough young man, although not particularly bright. He often gave Ciara some wildflowers or some other delight. The thought of headless Seamus at the dinner table gave Ciara the shivers.

So Ciara refused her mother's offer. Instead, the dead would be fed outside. When it was finally dark and the bonfires lit, Ciara took the pot of stew outside of her home and set it carefully on the ground. She placed a ladle and a bowl beside the pot. The dead could help themselves before beginning their journey. In case Seamus came by, Ciara left him a bunch of wildflowers.

For some, the festival began with the lighting of the bonfires. For Ciara, it would begin the next morning at daylight. In the meantime, Ciara remained safely in the house.

In years past, Ciara hid under the covers the entire night of Samhain. In no way did she wish to have any contact with the dead. But this year, Ciara managed the courage to look out of the window from time to time. She wanted to see if the dead really did begin their journey to the other world. She particularly wanted to see Aunt Mary and Seamus.

All of the stories she had heard her entire life turned out to be true! Ciara saw! With the light from the bonfires, she could see many dead people walking around in the village. She was sure they were dead, since they wore old tattered and blood-stained clothes. They also walked slowly and aimlessly, almost as if they had been drinking poitín. She had doubts a few times, when she thought she recognized some living neighbors dressed in clothes of the dead.

But all doubts vanished when she saw Aunt Mary!

There she was, in front of Ciara's house scooping out a ladle full of stew. Mary was almost as robust as the day she died. Ciara knew it was her Aunt Mary. She wore the same cloak she always wore, with the hood covering up most of her face. Ciara couldn't see her full face, but sure looked like Aunt Mary otherwise. Ciara didn't have enough courage to say anything. She simply watched Aunt Mary eat the stew and waddle away.

Not long after that, Seamus arrived!

He was tall – he seemed to be as tall as he was before he lost his head. He always wore the fur of a bear on his shoulders when he went into battle. Tonight, the bear fur covered everything except Seamus' helmet, which rested firmly on his shoulders. Seamus went to the door and gathered a full ladle of stew.

Ciara couldn't resist asking Seamus a question: "Seamus, you're headless. How's that working out for you, seeing as how you didn't use it much when you were alive?"

Seamus didn't respond, but ambled off into the village carrying the wildflowers with him. Ciara shouted out, as Seamus walked away:

"Seamus, don't forget to send us a message once you get to Ohio."

Postscript

After publication of my first book, a good friend asked: "Are there any zombies in the book?"

Since that book was non-fiction, I had to answer, "No!"

To which he replied: "How do you expect to sell a book in this day and age if it doesn't have any zombies?"

My friend is about 90% fruitcake and 10% genius, so I had to wonder whether his comments came from the fruitcake or the genius side of his brain. To hedge my bets, I included a zombie story to this book.

This is an original story about Samhain, the ancient Celtic festival celebrating the end of the harvest season and the beginning of the new year. By our modern calendar, Samhain was celebrated in late October or early November.

If you know anything about the Irish, you know that an Irishman will never pass up anything free. As you may have gleaned from the story, many an Irishman dressed up as a dead person on Samhain in order to eat the free food. The holiday has evolved a bit, but we still celebrate it in modern times -- on October 31st as Halloween.

I apologize to all Buckeyes. I had to give a name to a terrible place, and being a Michigan Wolverine, I had to call the place where no living person would ever wish to go "Ohio".

R. WILKINSON.
WHISKEY
XXX

The Connemara Fishermen

Most men in Connemara are skillful in the art of fishing. But there are, at least, two men who are not. These two men met a third man, who was indeed a skilled angler, at a pub one evening. Fishermen, as a rule, are more than willing to boast about fish caught, and sometimes even admit to the fish lost. But they are, as an equal rule, tight-lipped as to the where, the when, and the how. They simply do not wish others to catch fish from their best fishing spots. This third man, though, had more than a pint or two and became very specific in his discussions.

"The best fish," he said, "are in the River Owenglin. The biggest of the fish lurk around the big bend in the river, which truth be told, is not far from the pub in which we are sitting. And the fish are the hungriest, and the easiest to catch, early in the morn just as the sun begins to rise."

That was all the two Connemara men needed to hear. The next morning they were out of bed by 4:00 am and at the river by half past. It is chilly in early morning so they each brought with them a pint of Tullamore D.E.W. They understood, as do we all, that a nip of Irish whiskey takes the chill off the bones. They each took a nip as soon as they reached the river.

Connemara   Conn-ee-MAR-ah

They found a boat on the bank of the river, which they reckoned they could borrow for a few hours. It did not take them very long to reach the big bend in the river. Delighted to be there, and to celebrate the fish they were about to catch, they each took another drink from the pint. Or maybe it was two drinks, who's to say.

The current of the River Owenglin is pretty strong at the bend. By the time the two fishermen finished a drink or two of the pint, the river current pushed them further downstream. This forced the two men to row back upstream to the river bend, and they brought the oars out of the water and prepared to fish. The extra work called for another nip or two and, in the time it took for the few more, the current took them back downstream.

The two fishermen spent most of the morning rowing upstream to the river bend, taking a drink or two of whiskey once they got there, and flowing downstream with the current, and repeating the process yet again. Indeed, the two spent the entire morning on the river without ever getting fishing lines into the water.

By noon or so, the two men were tired and hungry. They were also quite angry. They'd been on the river all morning and had yet to catch a fish! They began to wonder if their friend had been pulling their leg, when he told them that the fishing was so good at this river bend.

The two decided to take a break for lunch, and hoped the fishing would be better in the afternoon. They rowed to a nearby village, docked the boat at the village pier, and went into the nearest pub. They asked the owner of the pub what he had on the menu.

The owner said: "I have a special soup with a sandwich, and I have a special sandwich with soup."

One fisherman said "I'll have the special soup with a sandwich plus a glass of Tullamore."

The other fisherman said "I'll have the special sandwich with the soup and I'll have a glass as well."

The pub owner soon brought each fisherman a sandwich and bowl of soup. And, as you might have guessed, there wasn't any difference between the two servings. They also each had a glass of whiskey which was refilled two or three times before they left the pub.

They stopped at an Off Licence liquor shop on the way to the pier, since, of course, it would be cold on the water and they needed something to ward off the cold.

Somehow they were able to find the boat. They untied it from the pier, and rowed to the middle of the river. They couldn't remember, though, which way to go. They had a fifty-fifty chance of going back to their fishing spot, since the river only went two ways.

They chose the downriver path, since it is much easier to row a boat down river than up. The bend, where they fished all morning, was unfortunately up river. They never did make it there.

The current remained strong and took them to the south bank of the river. They managed to row the boat back to the middle, but the current pushed them to the north bank. They continued down the river, bouncing from the south bank to the north along the way. They somehow managed to get their lines in the water, in between drinks of whiskey.

They still were not able to catch a fish, and they became quite belligerent about it. They started to argue, each one blaming the other for scaring away the fish, or for crashing into the bank.

Late in the afternoon, they gave up on the fishing altogether. They weren't exactly sure where they were, but they did see a small village further downstream. They continued to bounce from river bank to river bank until they made it to the village. Somehow, they docked the boat, although they got a little wet in the process.

It was a long day and they were exhausted. Fishing and rowing and fishing and rowing. It was a lot of work. They thought they needed to reward themselves.

So they went into the nearest pub.

They were in the pub quite a while. They even went through multiple mood changes. They sang and danced with the other patrons at the pub. They also argued about the lack of fish and whose fault that was.

It was finally time to leave. There is in fact somewhat of a debate on this issue. It is not at all clear whether the two fishermen decided to leave the pub, or whether the pub owner threw them out. In either event, they left the pub.

They walked out of the village, although they didn't pay much attention to which direction they were heading. They didn't know which way was home anyway.

When they got out of town, they were on a narrow, one lane dirt path.

Suddenly, one of the fishermen said: "Oh my Lord. We were at the pub all night!"

The other said: "Don't be daft. It's still early."

"Early? Early, you say? The sun has already come out."

"Sun? What sun ye be talking about?"

"That sun there", he said as he pointed to the sky. And the sky was indeed quite bright.

"Bullocks. That's not the sun. That's the moon!"

"No, that's the sun, not the moon".

"No, it's the moon, you moron."

And the argument continued. "It's the sun".

"No, it's the moon".

Back and forth.

The argument turned to blows, or at least sort of. Neither one of them could land a punch. One man swung at the other and missed. The other swung back, and he too missed. They were both a little challenged in the coordination department by this time.

Since they couldn't do much in the way of boxing, one grabbed the other and they began to wrestle. They were soon on the ground, rolling around back and forth to no particular advantage, and causing no damage at all. But still yelling all the while.

"It's the sun."

"No it's the moon."

"You idjit, it's the sun."

"Bullocks, it's the moon"

Eventually, the two men ended up flat on their backs. Both looking up at the sky. They were, by now, exhausted. They were no longer yelling, but the discussion continued.

"Do you want to go fishing again tomorrow?"

"Of course. It was your fault we didn't catch anything today."

"Mine? You had the oars. I don't think you missed a bank in the river all afternoon."

"You were too busy with your bottle to help at all".

The two men paused for a while, still flat on their backs.

One of them finally said: "And I still say it's the sun".

"And I still say it's the moon."

A short while later, another man walked down the same path. He saw the two men lying on the ground and was a wee bit concerned. He asked them: "Are you two men all right?"

"Aye", one of them said. "We're fine. But would you, kind sir, settle an argument for us?"

"I will certainly try", said the stranger.

"Well then please look up into the sky," said one fisherman while still lying on his back.

And so the stranger looked straight up to the sky.

And the other fisherman asked: "Is that the sun ye be looking at, or is that the moon?"

The stranger looked at the two men, then back into the sky, and then back at the two men.

"I'm sorry boys, but I cannot help you," he said. Adding:

"I'm afraid I'm not from around here."

Postscript

This is a much elaborated version of a joke I heard in a pub in Ireland. I couldn't resist retelling it, and building it into a full story. I placed the story in Connemara simply because I love the region. It has wonderful rivers, streams and a few lakes. So of course I built the story around two fishermen.

The fishermen's experience on the river is, as best as I can remember, a true story in which I was a participant.

R.I.P
MCLAIN
R.WILKINSON.

The Spaewife And The Barnacle Geese

Lauchlan MacIain was an ambitious man. He was chief of the MacIains of Ardnamurchan, ruler of Scotland's Ardnamurchan peninsula and the nearby Isle of Mull. But he wanted more, and his ambitions led him to the spaewife and the home of the barnacle geese.

The MacIains descended from Iain MacDonald. Iain's father and his two brothers were each, at one time or another, the Lord of the Isles. That title always belonged to the head of Clan Donald – chief of the clan and all of its allied clans. The Lord of the Isles ruled the west coast of Scotland, the northeast coast of Ireland, and the Hebrides Islands in between. That domain included Ardnamurchan and the Isle of Mull.

The MacIains remained a part of Clan Donald for many generations, although the two branches of the family were often at odds. Like the time the McIains abducted John MacDonald and his sons from Ireland, after which they were taken to Edinburgh and hanged.

Spaewife *SPAY-wife* or *spe-WIFE*
Lauchlan *LOCK-lin*
Ardnamurchan *AR-din-ah-MER-kin*
Hebrides *HEB-bree-dees*
Edinburgh *ED-in-burra*
Isla *EYE-la*
Pollag acraich *POLL-ag-ah-CRAY*
Neil Neonach *NEIL NEE-nahk*
Cnoc na Aighlean *KNOCK –na-AYE-lan*
Loch Gruinart *LOCK – GROO-nyart*
Dubh Sith *DOO Shee*

Such is the nature of family squabbles, and all was soon forgiven although not, by any means, forgotten.

The island of Isla was the center of the Clan Donald world. But Lauchlan McIain wanted Isla. The King of Scotland said that Lauchlan could have it. The MacDonalds did not give it up. So Lauchlan decided to take it. Lauchlan McIain assembled his army and several ships, and planned his invasion of Isla.

But first he sought the advice of the Isle of Mull's only spaewife. She, like any spaewife, could see into the future. No wise man of Mull would ever embark upon anything of importance without first seeking the advice of the island's spaewife. She was indeed a vivid seer of the future.

Lauchlan brought with him a cow for the spaewife in payment. She usually accepted far less for her services. But a look into a future of Lauchlan's ambitious plan was important — important enough indeed to be paid for with a cow. He left the cow within the fenced area around the spaewife's croft house and entered her home.

"I know why ye are here, and why ye brought me a cow," said the spaewife. "I also know what will happen to ye when your army invades Isla."

"Well woman, if you know what will happen then tell me," responded Lauchlan.

"Ye'll meet the Clan Donald army on Isla and you will defeat them. But it is my advice you must heed," said the spaewife.

"What, pray tell, is your advice?" asked Lauchlan.

The spaewife leaned toward Lauchlan and lowered her voice to barely a whisper. She said to Lauchlan: "Ye must not, under any circumstance of any kind or manner, land your ships at Pollag Acraich – the Anchorage Pool".

"Aye then, I will not do so," said Lauchlan.

The spaewife was not finished, and added: "And also, ye must not, under any circumstance of any kind or manner, drink – or allow your men to drink – water at Neil Neonach – Strange Neil."

"Aye, there is plenty of water on Isla and we shall not drink at Strange Neil," said Lauchlan.

"And last," said the spaewife, "ye must not, under any circumstance of any kind or manner, plant your battle flag at Cnoc na Aighlean - Hind's Hill."

"Aye as well," said Lauchlan, "for there are many other places to fight the battle."

Lauchlan left the spaewife satisfied that the advice was well worth the price of a cow.

Armed with the spaewife's vision of the future, Lauchlan and his army set sail for Isla. It was a hot August day in 1598 when they arrived.

Lauchlan was a wee bit worried about the spaewife's first warning, so he decided not to land at the usual island mooring spots. His ships sailed into a small bay and anchored off shore. His men got off of the boats and waded to shore, now ready for battle. The McIains saw a shepherd boy near shore, and asked him where they were.

The shepherd boy told them: "This is Pollag Acraich – the Anchorage Pool".

Lachlan said: "Damn it." But he decided to proceed with the invasion.

The MacIains marched for hours around the island of Isla, trying to find the Clan Donald army. By midday, they were parched and thirsty and began to look for fresh water. They came upon a well. All of the MacIains drank from the well and filled up their animal bladders with water for the rest of the day.

After they completed this task, a MacIain noticed a sign which had fallen from the well. The sign read –– "Neil Neonach" – Strange Neil.

Lachlan said: "Double damn it."

But with their collective thirst quenched, the MacIains marched on. Late in the afternoon they came upon a small hill. From the hilltop, they saw the Clan Donald army below. With the advantage of the high ground, Lauchlan decided that this would be a good place to begin the battle. Lauchlan ordered his battle flag planted at the top of the hill, and prepared his men for battle.

One of the MacIains told Lauchlan that this hill was called Cnoc nan Aighean, Hind's Hill. At this point, Lachlan should have gone home. But he was a stubborn man. His army was ready and the MacDonalds were finally in his sight.

The MacDonalds then did a strange thing. They started to march sideways. Then they marched forward. Then they marched backwards. Then sideways again.

Lauchlan was baffled by this, until he realized that the late afternoon sun was now directly in his eyes. The MacDonalds had marched around until they had the sun at their backs.

Lachlan decided it was time to end all of this – spaewife be damned, sun be damned. He ordered his first wave to attack.

His plan was a simple attempt to avoid crowding the entire MacIain army into the small space between the hill and the MacDonald army. The attack would thus be in two waves, with the half the army charging across that space and engaging the MacDonalds, followed shortly by the second half of the MacIain army.

It did not go according to plan. The MacDonalds repulsed the first wave of the attack. The MacIains in the first wave began to retreat just as the MacIains in the second wave began to attack. The two waves became completely entangled – the first wave couldn't retreat and the second wave couldn't attack.

The MacDonalds then attacked. With the McIain army entangled with each other, the battle turned into a rout.

The MacIains brought nearly three hundred men to Isla. All but thirty died in battle. These thirty men escaped and sought haven in the nearby Kilnave Chapel. Once inside, they bolted the doors and hoped the MacDonalds would respect the holy ground.

Alas, it was not to be. When the MacDonalds arrived, they set fire to the chapel's thatched roof. Trapped inside, all but one of the MacIains was burned to death. The sole survivor escaped the burning chapel and swam to a nearby island.

Lauchlan died at the foot of Hind's Hill. He was killed by a hunch-backed dwarf, which was fitting for a man who ignored the advice of a spaewife. Lauchlan's killer was Dubh Sith – Black Fairy – called that because of his extremely short stature and dark hairy body. The Black Fairy did not fit the normal image of a warrior, but he did have an equalizer – a small single shot pistol. In the course of the battle, Black Fairy shot Lauchlan MacIain in the head.

Thirty MacDonalds were killed. James, their chief, led the clan in this battle, and he received a chest wound. He was left for dead by his men. As it turns out, he wasn't dead at all. His men found him the next day. He recovered from his wound and lived for many more decades.

The battle was fought at a place called Loch Gruinart. It is now a bird sanctuary, known best as a winter home for barnacle geese.

So there is indeed a moral to this story.

If you seek the advice of a spaewife, then heed the advice.

Or else your final resting place will be a sanctuary for barnacle geese.

The battle between the MacIains and the MacDonalds on Isla is a true story, thoroughly researched and verified. The role the spaewife played in the whole affair falls in the category of "true legend", as does that of the Black Fairy.

Despite the name, Loch Gruinart is a bay and not a lake. The land on its three sides is owned by the Royal Society for the Protection of Birds and maintained as a bird sanctuary. Barnacle geese spend winters there and summers in Greenland.

SPIRITS ALES
TULLAMORE DEW
~R. WILKINSON~

Buy The Horse A Guinness

The horse was fine when Tara bought her. It was a mare with long, strong legs, easy temperament, and great bloodlines. She ran around the meadow without a care. The seller said that the horse never had any health issues of any kind. Tara was certain she would be a wonderful horse.

But when Tara brought the horse home and into the barn, things changed. The horse began to sneeze, became listless, and even developed a rash. No matter the amount of exercise, the horse did not sweat a drop.

Tara bemoaned to her husband: "I really don't know what to do with that horse. I've tried everything."

"I'll take him to Fafa's in the morning," Peadar responded.

"Don't be daft. You'll not be taking the horse to that pub," said Tara. "The horse needs a proper veterinarian."

"And who has the money for a proper veterinarian?" asked Peadar. "We spent all of our extra money on the horse."

"Yes, and that is why we need a proper cure!"

"Maybe and maybe not. What is for sure is that a vet will charge us more money than we have. Fafa will give me the answer for the cost of a pint of Guinness."

The couple argued for some time until they reached an understanding. They would take the horse into the village. They would stop first at the veterinarian's. They would take the horse to Fafa's if -- and only if -- the veterinarian failed

to find a cure.

Tara's confidence was with the vet. She had yet to

meet him but heard wonderful things about him. Everyone

in West Cork had. He was new to the area and was by all

accounts a brilliant young man. He was educated at Trinity

College and veterinarian school at University College

Dublin. No one with such training had ever treated the

animals in these parts. Surely he would be able to cure the

horse of its ailment.

Peadar's confidence was with Fafa, and not only

because he was less expensive. Everyone in West Cork

knew Fafa's pub, and would visit the pub from time to time.

There were other pubs in West Cork, of course, and they

all served the same array of beverages. Fafa's beer and

whiskey menu was the same as the other pubs. But it wasn't

the beverage menu that attracted patrons to Fafa's.

Nor was it the ambiance. Fafa's grandfather bought

the pub generations ago and never changed a thing. Neither

did Fafa's father, when he owned the pub, nor Fafa, now that the pub was his. Farm implements and a few other relics hung on the walls, all covered with several inches of dust. The sign above the pub's door read "Gus O'Riley's" and no one ever bothered to change the sign. No one ever called it by that name, though, and no one remembered a man named Gus O'Riley. Everyone knew the pub as "Fafa's".

It was neither the menu nor the décor that attracted patrons to Fafa's pub. It was Fafa himself.

Fafa was an elderly man of few words and even less education. He walked slowly behind the bar tending to customers. He spoke softly to those who spoke to him first. He disdained idle chit chat, but would respond to those who submitted an inquiry to him. And many of the patrons in Fafa's were there to do just that – submit an inquiry to Fafa.

Fafa had the reputation of knowing nearly everything about anything. Fafa could tell you each of the horses riding in the Derby this year, together with the jockey riding each and the odds of winning. Fafa knew of every eligible bachelor in West Cork looking for a lady, and every lady in West Cork looking for a husband. Fafa knew how to stop a high-strung dog from barking and how to turn a passive hound into a first-rate watch dog. Sly patrons often tried to stump Fafa with a question he could not answer. Few were successful.

Where Fafa got his information, nobody knew. He lived in the pub's back room and rarely left the building. He never went to school, as anyone could recall. He couldn't spell much and often mispronounced words. He didn't know the meaning of the word "research". Somehow, he just knew things.

Peadar thought it foolish to go to the vet before Fafa's, but Tara was insistent. They left home early and reached the village before noon. The veterinarian was in and saw the horse straight away.

The vet looked over the horse front to rear, poking and jabbing everywhere in between. He looked into the horse's eyes, mouth, ears, and rear. He looked especially close at the rash. He asked Tara and the horse a lot of questions throughout the examination, but only Tara answered.

"Well doctor, what's her problem?" Tara asked.

"I'm not quite sure yet," replied the vet. "The sneezing suggests an allergy. The rash suggests that she brushed up against something. The listlessness and absence of sweat suggests that something is going on internally. The combination of these is a bit of a puzzle. The horse may have picked up a parasite or perhaps an infection."

He added, "I suggest a few tests. I'll draw some blood, and take a stool and urine sample. We'll send all of this to the lab and see what turns up."

"How much will this cost?" Peadar wanted to know.

"Lab work can be expensive, and so might treatment once we figure out what is wrong", responded the vet.

"Before we spend any more money, doc, I'm going to take her to Fafa. He might know what to do for a lot less money," Peadar said.

Peadar and Tara argued a bit about this. The veterinarian was torn – he wanted the best care for his patient and couldn't magine the horse getting better care at a pub. But it wasn't his choice to make and if Peadar chose to take him to Fafa's, then so be it.

Peadar persisted and Tara gave in. Peadar led the horse out of the veterinarian's office, into the street, and down the road to Fafa's. He continued to lead the horse through the door, into the pub and up to the bar. Tara followed. The vet followed as well, for his curiosity got the best of him.

Fafa poured a pint of Guinness for Peadar, without saying a word. Fafa looked at Tara and asked, "What would you like?"

"I'll have the same," she said.

The vet added, "And I will as well."

Fafa poured a pint for Tara and yet another for the veterinarian. He then asked, "What does the horse want?"

"He wants whatever will cure him," said Peadar.

Fafa stared at the horse for several moments before asking: "Does the horse have a problem?"

"He sneezes, doesn't sweat much, has a rash, and is listless," says Peadar. "He wasn't that way before, least not that we are aware. It all started when we bought him and brought him to our barn."

Tara told Fafa the entire story of the perfectly fine horse, playful in the meadow, listless and sneezy in the barn. The horse sneezed throughout the story.

"Well," Fafa said, "I suggest that you buy the horse a Guinness."

"A Guinness? Really? You want me to buy the horse a pint of Guinness?" asked Peadar.

"Don't be foolish," replied Fafa. "It's a horse! She doesn't need a pint. She needs a bucket!"

Peadar went into his pocket, pulled out all the money he had, and placed it on the bar. He frankly did not know the cost of a bucket of Guinness. Fafa took some of the money and left the rest on the bar. He reached below the bar for a bucket.

Fafa held the bucket at a proper angle, partially filled it with Guinness from the tap, then placed the bucket on the floor. After what seemed like an eternity, he picked up the bucket, held it level this time, and filled it to the brim, although he released the Guinness much slower from the tap this time. Finally, he placed the bucket on the bar in front of the horse.

The horse took a slurp. Liked it and took another. It wasn't long before the bucket was empty.

Within moments, the sneezing stopped. The horse started to sweat. The rash went away. The horse got frisky and knocked over the bar stool.

"Bring her in for another bucket of Guinness once in a while and the horse will be fine," said Fafa.

Peadar was not at all surprised, fully expecting Fafa to know the cure. Tara was delighted that her horse appeared cured.

The veterinarian was skeptical, saying. "I doubt that you've given this horse a permanent cure. And if you have, it was a lucky guess."

"Not at all, and it was quite obvious for all to see," said Fafa.

"How so?" asked the vet.

"The horse was fine in the meadow and showed symptoms only when put in the barn. What was in the barn that wasn't in the meadow? Hay, of course. The horse is allergic to hay!" said Fafa.

"The hay caused the sneezing and the rash," Fafa added. "The hay also caused her to stop normal sweating. Her listless nature was her reaction to the rest."

"That was the problem?" asked the veterinarian.

"Aye. All we needed to do," said Fafa, "was take away the hay and replace it with barley. The only barley I have in my pub is in the whiskey and in the Guinness. I didn't expect Peadar to buy a bucket of whiskey, so I sold him a bucket of Guinness."

"So the only treatment necessary," said the veterinarian as he drank his own pint, "was to buy the horse a Guinness!"

Postscript

This story's essence was developed at a workshop I conducted at the Irish Music Festival in Ocean Shores, Washington. I invited participants to describe people, places, conflicts, themes, and the like, hoping to illustrate and enhance descriptive skills. Before we realized it, we had the elements of a good story!

We didn't write the story at the workshop, but we all left the session satisfied that we collectively created something special. We were all surprised at how well the process worked.

Later, I put together the elements of the story into the version you just read. We generated some other ideas which I didn't weave into this story. I added a few of my own twists as well.

By the way, I've frequented one of Ireland's best pubs referred to by the locals as "Fafa's". That is not the pub name on the outside sign, but no one in town knows the pub by any other name.

R.WILKINSON

The Wiser Adviser To The King

No Irish king earned more respect and admiration from his people than Brian Bóruma. He was, for a time, King of Thomond – an ancient kingdom in southern Ireland. He later became King of Munster – the southern quarter or so of the island. Ultimately, he became High King of all of Ireland.

As king, he was often called upon to settle disputes among the clans of Ireland. This was, perhaps, his most important task. Were it not for the king's ability to resolve such disputes, competing clans would be in a constant state of warfare.

While King of Thomond, Brian had two trusted advisers. He counted on both of them whenever he faced a difficult decision. This made the two advisers powerful men, since they could influence the fate of the kingdom. The advisers were Ruaidrí and Angus.

Most recently, Brian tended to follow the advice of Ruaidrí and ignore that of Angus. This made Angus extremely jealous, he being a person easily made so. But Angus was not only jealous, he was ambitious. He thought that if he could get rid of, or at least discredit, Ruaidrí, then Angus would be the number one adviser to the king and the second most powerful person in the kingdom.

Bóruma   Bore-oo (as in "pool")
Ruaidrí   Rory

So Angus hatched a plot, which he implemented the next time the king called upon him and Ruaidri to lend advice. This took place at a banquet in the Village of Sneem filled with dozens of important local clan chiefs. Two different clans claimed the right to graze cattle along a local river, and the chiefs argued hard and loud in support of their claims. Finally, Brian was called upon to make a decision.

Brian then asked his advisers, "What do my most trusted advisers think?"

Before Ruaidri could answer, Angus shouted out: "I think you should listen to my advice, and not that of Ruaidri. I can prove to you, and before all of the clan chiefs, that I am the better adviser."

Brian was surprised at such a claim, being unaware of any discord among his trusted advisers. He then asked, "How do you propose to do that?"

"I challenge Ruaidri to answer three of my questions. I guarantee that he cannot," Angus replied.

"This might be interesting", said Brian. "Please proceed to ask your questions three."

So Angus asked Ruaidri: "How many stars are there in the sky?"

Ruaidri thought about this for a moment. It was daylight at the time and he certainly could not count the stars even if it were night.

Ruaidri then commanded: "Bring me a sheep!"

Someone brought a sheep into the banquet hall.

Ruaidri then said: "There are as many stars in the sky as there are hairs on this sheep. You may count them if you wish to verify my answer."

Brian laughed. He then said: "I think your answer is sufficient. Angus, ask your second question."

Angus was surprised that Ruaidri could answer the first question, but remained confident that the second could not be correctly answered.

Angus then said: "Here is my second question. Where is the center of the earth?"

Ruaidrí did not hesitate at all: "The answer is quite simple."

Ruaidrí pulled his sword out of his scabbard. He pointed the sword to the floor of the banquet hall and carved a line on the floor.

He then said: "This line is the center of the earth."

Ruaidrí stood on the line and turned to his left. "Half of the earth is on this side."

He then turned around and faced the other way. "And half of the earth is on this side."

Brian laughed again, even louder than before. "I always thought that I was the center of the earth. And now I know that it is true!"

By now, Angus was getting a wee bit worried. He began to sweat. His hands twitched nervously. He knew that the king was leaning even more towards Ruaidrí.

"I have one more question", said Angus.

"Ask your third question", said the king, "and it better be a good one!"

So Angus asked, "How many human beings are there in Ireland?"

Ruaidrí replied: "It would be an easy task to count all of the human beings in Ireland. But alas, your question is a difficult one to answer."

"For there are many creatures," Ruaidrí continued, "who are like you Angus and cannot be easily classified as human or not. It is only if you and all like you are banished from this island that one can count the exact number of humans there are in Ireland."

With that Brian said: "I have heard enough! Angus, you are indeed a creature of unknown origin. I banish you from our kingdom. I do not need your advice any longer."

Angus was too clever and too ambitious for his own good. He went from a trusted adviser to Brian to a creature banished from the kingdom forever.

Little is known about what happened to Angus thereafter. It is often said that he spent the rest of his days as a beggar on the Isle of Skye off the coast of Scotland.

It is almost as often said that Angus was quite prolific while in Scotland. This might explain why, to this day, there are so many souls there who go by the name "Angus".

Ruaidri, on the other hand, remained in Ireland and became the wiser adviser to the king.

Postscript

This is my take on another old tale, and I've retold it a many times and never quite the same way twice. I first told it in Ireland at a pub in the Village of Sneem, which is within the ancient Kingdom of Thomond and the modern County Kerry. So in this version, I set the tale in Sneem and made Brian the story's king.

Lochlann The Leprechaun

We all know about leprechauns. Some people think they are a lot like Bigfoot. But there is a difference between a Bigfoot and a leprechaun.

There are, truth be told, two differences. A Bigfoot has big feet, hence the name. A leprechaun has wee little feet.

The other difference is that a Bigfoot is the figment of the active imagination of some foolish people who like to chase mythical creatures. Leprechauns, in contrast, exist! Leprechauns have been around in Ireland for thousands of years. There is at least one leprechaun in New Mexico, the state aptly called "The Land of Enchantment".

Leprechaun comes from two old Irish words - lú meaning small and orpán meaning body. They are, indeed, very mysterious creatures. They are thought to descend from Tuatha Dé or Tribe of the Gods. Some say that the leprechaun is the offspring of an evil spirit and a degenerate fairy. This may or may not be true. If it is, then it is proof that some girls just want to have fun.

There are many curious facts about leprechauns. One is that there are no female leprechauns. All leprechauns are male! Nor is there

Lochlann *LOCK-lin*
Saoirse *SEER-sha* or *SIR-sha*
Armagh *ar-MAH*
Jemez *HAY-mez*

evidence of leprechauns being capable of asexual reproduction, which is not much fun in any event.

So if there are no women leprechauns, and if asexual reproduction is not an option, where did the leprechauns come from? Maybe the legend of the evil spirits and degenerate fairies isn't so farfetched.

Since most fairies are straight-laced, proper women, there are not many degenerate fairies reproducing with evil spirits. That explains why there are so few leprechauns.

Those that do exist have been around a long, long time. They are, with very few exceptions, old men. Very, very old men.

Small old men. They are not the wee characters portrayed in cartoons or Lucky Charms commercials. They are about the size of young boys. A meter or so tall.

Leprechauns are not evil, per se. As by-products of evil spirits and degenerate fairies, they are neither wholly good nor wholly evil. But there is a dominant characteristic of old men. Old men are crotchety. Short tempered, set in their ways, grumpy, grouchy, crabby, cranky, and irritable. All old men are that way. Try to imagine an old man who is perhaps a thousand years old - he'd be much worse.

Now try to imagine an old man who has never been with a woman for a thousand years. He'd be much, much worse. It brings a whole meaning to the word crotchety.

Leprechauns like to be left alone and are happiest when they are so. They do however love to party with other leprechauns. They are adept at the tin whistle and fiddle, and love to dance. They have been known to wear out shoes regularly from so much dancing. This explains why leprechauns are skilled shoemakers.

Leprechauns do have some magical powers. This comes from the degenerate fairy side of the family. If a person is lucky enough to capture one, a leprechaun might use his magic to negotiate his freedom.

All of this leads us to the true story of Lochlann the leprechaun and Saoirse the orphan girl. The story takes place in the middle 1800's, shortly after the Great Hunger.

Lochlann lived in a heavily forested region of County Armagh. Lochlann kept pretty much to himself. By the middle 1800's, he was about 950 years old, give or take a decade or two.

Saoirse survived the blight of the potato and the famine fevers which killed so many, including her family. Saoirse moved into a hovel, vacated by a family who left for America. She got by from handouts from some neighbors and by scavenging for food in the nearby forest.

It was on one of the scavengings, while picking wild blueberries, that Saoirse heard the sound of a tin whistle in the distance. She quietly moved in the direction of the music, taking several minutes to make her way closer to the sound. Then she stopped and saw him. There he was, only a few feet away. Oblivious to her, and totally immersed with his whistle, sat Lochlann the leprechaun.

Saoirse knew the powers of the leprechaun from stories, but had never seen one in real life. Legend had it that a leprechaun will grant you three wishes in exchange for his freedom. Saoirse, being no fool, decided to test the legend.

She leaped towards the leprechaun, and grabbed him by the foot. She was a slightly built lass, barely over six stone in weight and five feet in height. The wee leprechaun was only about three feet tall and three stone and, after all, was nearly a thousand years old. Lochlann was no match for Saoirse and she quickly subdued him.

With the struggle complete, Lochlann said: "Please do not hurt me. I only want to be left alone. I promise you, I will grant you three wishes if you set me free."

Saoirse replied, "I will set you free AFTER you've granted my three wishes and not before."

"That's not how it works," protested Lochlann. "I will grant you three wishes AFTER you set me free."

Lochlann was clearly not used to dealing with women. Any man will tell you "There is no negotiating with a woman". Lochlann eventually realized this.

So he asked: "What, then, is your first wish?"

Saoirse said: "I wish to go to America. There I will marry an Irish man. All of the good Irish men have gone to America. So take me to America."

Lochlann replied: "I will grant you your first wish".

And so Lochlann and Saoirse walked out of the Armagh forest and north to Belfast. From there they took the first boat to Liverpool. Once in Liverpool, they boarded a ship which had brought cotton from New Orleans to Liverpool and the huge English linen mills. In Liverpool, the ship was refitted with bunk beds and filled up with Irish for the return trip to New Orleans.

Saoirse covered Lochlann in a cloak so that other passengers would not realize that he was a leprechaun. The few people who saw his face through the cloak merely thought he was an ugly boy and Saoirse's younger brother. He wasn't bad looking, as leprechauns go, but for those who thought he was a young boy, he was extremely ugly. The two boarded the ship, and eight weeks later they were in New Orleans.

And so Lochlann asked: "What, then, is your second wish?"

Saoirse said: "I wish to marry an Irish man. He must be young, strong, and handsome. Please will you find me such an Irish man?"

Lochlann replied: "I grant your second wish."

Lochlann went immediately to the wharf of the Port of New Orleans. There he saw slaves from Africa and Irish men carrying bales of cotton, and loading them aboard ships bound for Liverpool. Lochlann saw a handsome young man. He was tall and strong. After some inquiry, Lochlann realized that the young man was indeed an Irishman in the market for a wife. His name was Peter.

Peter was very slow in speech and it was soon clear in conversation that he was not the brightest star in the galaxy, but Lochlann thought he would do. Lochlann brought Peter to meet Saoirse.

Peter and Saoirse talked for some time, until Saoirse turned to Lochlann and said: "He's a wee bit of a dimwit".

Lochlann said: "You asked for an Irish man who was young, strong and handsome, and willing to marry you. You didn't say anything about him being smart."

Saoirse agreed, and soon thereafter she and Peter were married in New Orleans. Lochlann was the best man, although the couple told the priest that Lochlann was the "best boy".

After the wedding, Lochlann asked: "What is your third wish?"

Saoirse said: "I have lived my entire life in Ireland, where it rains almost every day. Indeed, we only know 'tis summer because the rain gets warmer. My third wish is to live the rest of my days with Peter in a place in which it rarely rains."

Lochlann replied: "I grant you your third wish."

And so the three of them began a long journey to the west, walking all of the way. They traveled for weeks on end until they reached a land as far from water as land could be.

There they found another traveler and asked "What is this placed called?"

The traveler said "This place is called Texas".

Saoirse said: "Oh no, this will not do. I have no desire to live in Texas."

The three kept heading west. They reached a place occupied by Navajo people and by a few Spanish missionaries. The place had a small trading post, deep in the New Mexico Territory, with a beautiful river running through it. The place was otherwise quite dry, it being in the desert, and not at all like Ireland.

"What is this placed called?" Saoirse asked.

"This place is the town of Aztec in the Territory of New Mexico" one man at the trading post said. "Someday, we will be in our own state, and we will call it New Mexico. It will be a wonderful state and we will refer to it as the Land of Enchantment. And the best thing about New Mexico is that it is not Texas.”

What is this river called?” Saoirse asked.

“It is the Rio de las Animas,” said the man, “although some call it Rio de las Animas Perdidas. It means River of Souls or, perhaps, River of Lost Souls.”

Saoirse continued her questioning: “How do you know that this will someday be a state?”

And the man replied: “Not far from here is a place they call the Four Corners. It is a place where four states meet. If New Mexico doesn’t become a state, they would have to call it Two or Three Corners, and that doesn’t make any sense.”

Saoirse replied: “I am no longer a lost soul, but I am enchanted with the Land of Enchantment and the future State of New Mexico. I wish to live here forever.”

“This will be your home, and now I have granted you three wishes,” Lochlann said. “It is time for you to set me free.”

Saoirse and Peter lived the rest of their days in Aztec along the River de las Animas. This portion of the world did indeed become the State of New Mexico. The two of them were born in Ireland, lived a while in New Orleans, and died after a long life in Aztec, New Mexico. They were both buried at the Aztec Cemetery on Chamisa Street.

Lochlann, unlike Saoirse, did not want anything to do with the desert. He meandered around for years, looking for land that reminded him, at least a wee bit, of Ireland.

Months of roaming finally led Lochlann to a heavily forested and hilly region. Lochlann didn't know it, but these hills were the Jemez Mountains. Lochlann, in fact, is still there. He's now a century over a thousand years old.

If you hike in the Jemez and are particularly quiet, you might hear the distinctive sound of an Irish tin whistle playing a tune such as "The Road to Lisdoonvarna". It would be played by none other than Lochlann the leprechaun.

Many in the Jemez have heard it — solid evidence indeed that leprechauns do exist -- in Ireland and in New Mexico.

Postscript

This is an original story, which I first told at a Celtic festival in Aztec, New Mexico, and hence the setting for a portion of the story.

I've been asked many times at similar festivals to tell a story about leprechauns. I didn't know many good leprechaun stories, so I made this one up.

·R·WILKINSON·

The Apprentice & The Baker

A young apprentice lived in a small village in County Donegal. He earned a wage from his employer while learning his trade, but it was barely enough to pay for the rent. The apprentice lived in one room above the only bakery in the village. The room had but one window, and just enough space for his bedroll and meager belongings.

His employer often provided a modest lunch. It wasn't much since the employer didn't have much in the way of food, or money for that matter, and the apprentice had the same lunch as his employer. When he did have a lunch, it was, most of the time, the apprentice boy's only meal of the day.

Once in a while the apprentice had enough money to buy some food. Sometimes someone in the village would give him some – an egg, or some left-over stew, or a potato or two. That was about it.

The bakery below the apprentice was operated by a very talented man who made some of the best baked goods in Donegal. He baked bread and made pastries and cookies, but he was most well-known for his cakes. People came to the village from miles away just for the delight of the baker's cakes. When the baker baked his cakes, the aroma spilled out into the street and the entire village. Everyone enjoyed the wonderful aroma of the cakes in the air.

The baker usually sold everything that he made, but he was very particular about the freshness of his baked goods. If something didn't sell on the day he made it, he threw it away. He refused to give anything away, for fear that people would wait for his free, day-old baked goods rather than buy his fresh baked goods. So instead, he dug a small pit behind the bakery and, from time to time, threw the stale baked goods into the pit.

The apprentice saw the baker do this once, and once was all it took. Every day, after the baker closed shop, the apprentice snuck behind the bakery and dug up the day-old stale bread. The old bread provided the apprentice with the sustenance he needed.

There was only one problem with the stale bread — it was stale bread! It had no flavor and no aroma. It was not a delight to eat. The apprentice ate it anyway, because he was hungry and he didn't have anything else to eat.

The apprentice usually left for work before the baker did his baking. One morning, though, the apprentice was late. While the apprentice was getting ready, he smelled a wonderful aroma coming from the bakery below. It was the baker, already at work and baking his cakes. The aroma of the cakes seeped in from the floor below and easily found its way into the nostrils of the apprentice. To the poor apprentice, this was perhaps as close to heaven as he could be.

The apprentice rushed to the window and opened it up. To his great delight, the aroma of the cakes filled the street and rose up from the bakery and into his window.

He then had a brilliant idea! The apprentice still had some bread left over from the day before. He took his remaining stale bread and held it outside the window. Within moments, the stale, day-old bread absorbed the aroma from the cakes. And the longer he held out the bread, the more aroma it absorbed.

When the apprentice could take it no longer, he pulled the bread back from outside the window and into his room. He took one bite of the bread and it was brilliant. It absorbed so much of the aroma from the cake that it tasted almost as good as the cake itself. The apprentice had the most delicious breakfast he ever had.

The apprentice followed this practice for many weeks, until he had nearly completed his apprenticeship. At night, he found some stale bread behind the bakery. In the morning, he held his bread outside of the window until it had soaked in the aroma from the baker's cakes. He then enjoyed this brilliant breakfast before going to work.

One morning, the baker walked outside of his shop at the exact moment the apprentice held bread outside of the window. Per chance, the baker looked up, and saw the arm of the apprentice holding a slice of bread through the window. It suddenly dawned on the baker that the bread was soaking in the aroma from his cakes.

It never did occur to the baker that the slice of bread held by the apprentice was a slice of stale bread which the baker had thrown away the day before.

But the baker shouted up to the apprentice: "Boy, you come down here this instant."

The apprentice complied, after eating his slice of bread, and went down the stairs into the street.

"I saw what you were doing," the baker yelled. "You were stealing the aroma from my cakes."

The apprentice admitted this, and said: "Yes, I was using the aroma from your cakes to improve the flavor of my bread. But I did not know that this was a crime."

"It certainly is", said the baker. "You were using the aroma of my cakes without paying for it. You have likely been doing this for days and days. You owe me money for stealing my aroma. I'm taking you to see the magistrate."

The baker then grabbed the apprentice by the ear, and led him down the street towards the village magistrate.

The village magistrate was a well-respected, but feared man. He heard all of the criminal cases in the village, as well as all civil disputes. He had the power to evict a tenant, and thus render someone homeless. He could order someone to jail in a criminal case, or order the defendant transported to Australia. If one could not pay a debt, the magistrate could send the debtor to prison - since such was, at the time, a crime.

The magistrate was in session on that particular morning. The baker stomped into the courtroom, still pulling the young apprentice by the ear.

"I demand justice," the baker said.

"And it is justice you shall receive", said the magistrate, "but you will have to wait your turn. I have a few other matters to resolve first."

It was nearly an hour before the magistrate was ready to hear the case brought by the baker.

"What seems to be the problem?" asked the magistrate.

"I am the village baker and I own the bakery in town."

"I am quite familiar with your bakery," said the magistrate, "but why is this young man in my courtroom."

"He is the tenant in the room above my bakery. I caught him in the act of stealing from me."

"And what is it that he stole from you?" asked the magistrate.

"He stole the aroma from my cakes" said the baker. "I caught him with his arm out the window with a piece of bread, soaking the bread in the aroma of my cakes."

"He did not pay for the aroma," the baker continued. "He probably has been doing this for God knows how long. He must pay me for the aroma which he has stolen from me!"

"This is serious. Quite serious indeed," said the magistrate. He then turned to the apprentice, and said: "What do you have to say for yourself?"

"I did, your honor, use the aroma of the cakes to make my meager rations tastier," said the apprentice, pleading: "I did not know that this was against the law".

"Well, I have no choice but to find you guilty as charged," said the magistrate. "You used the aroma from the baker's cakes without paying for them."

"But I am a poor apprentice and have but two ha-pennies to my name", said the apprentice.

Ha-penny HAY-pen-ee

"Then you shall pay two ha-pennies to the baker for using the aroma of his cakes," ruled the magistrate.

The baker smiled, quite pleased with the ruling. Two ha-pennies wasn't much, but at least he would be paid something. And perhaps others would be deterred from stealing aroma from his bakery.

The young apprentice reached into his right pocket. He dug deep into the pocket before he found one ha-penny. He took out the coin and dropped it on the table in front of him. He then dug deep into his left pocket until he found yet another ha-penny. He took this coin out and dropped it on the table. Both ha-pennies made the familiar sound of coins bouncing on a table.

The magistrate then said to the apprentice: "Now that you have placed two ha-pennies on the table, you may pick them up and put them back into your pockets."

The apprentice did as he was told and returned each coin to his pocket.

"I must protest," shouted the baker. "You found him guilty of stealing the aroma from my cakes. I am entitled to be paid!"

To which, the magistrate responded: "If you may charge the apprentice for the aroma of your cakes, then he may pay you with the sound of his money!"

Postscript

This is my version of an old, old tale. I've seen many versions of this and several references as to its origin. I won't even render a guess as to its origin but I love the parable just the same. My biggest twist was to change the setting to a small Irish village and a thoroughly Irish setting.

BARBER
R·WILKINSON·

The Annual Killing Of A Barber

Leary Lorc was King of Leinster and of the Irish "people of the land". These Celts were one of the first Celtic ethnic groups to move to Ireland. While in Europe, the people of the land – who the Romans called Dumnonii – stayed a few steps ahead of the ever-expanding Roman Empire. They lived in northern France before many moved across the channel to Ireland.

Leary's reign only lasted two years. Leary had a younger brother named Cova. Cova was a devious and jealous man who desperately wanted to become king. To do so, he needed to dispose of Leary. He also needed to get rid of Leary's son Alill, and Alill's mute son Loughra.

First to deal with Leary. Cova pretended to be dying. He spent all of his time in his bedroom, faking a fever. Word spread throughout the kingdom, and Leary trekked to Cova's home to pay a visit to the deathbed of his brother.

Leary entered the bedroom and leaned over his brother, as if to kiss him goodbye.

Leary said to his dying brother: "Unlucky is your illness".

Leary Lorc *LEER-rey LORK*
Dumnonii *Dah-MOAN-yi*
Cova *KAH-va*
Alill *AHL-yill*
Loughra *LOUW-ra*
Moriath *MOHR-ah*

Cova pulled a knife, which he had hidden under his pillow. He stabbed his elder brother to death.

Alill accompanied Leary on the visit, but waited outside of Cova's room so that Leary could have a private goodbye to his dying brother. While waiting, Cova's servant offered Alill liquid refreshment. Cova had already poisoned the drink and Alill died after his first gulp.

With Leary and Alill dead, Cova declared himself king.

There remained the matter of what to do with Loughra. Loughra was still a young boy. It was against Celtic law to kill a child who was somehow defective and a child who could not speak qualified. It was perfectly acceptable to kill a brother and a nephew, legally speaking. But Cova had to spare Loughra's life.

To insult Loughra forever, Cova forced Loughra to eat the heart of his grandfather, Leary.

And to eat the heart of his father, Alill.

And to eat a live mouse.

It is not at all obvious which one of these was the most disgusting to Loughra.

Cova exiled Loughra and Loughra's mother and they both moved to Brittany in northern France. Certainly Loughra much preferred the French cuisine.

While still a child, though, Loughra played a game of hurling with other Brittany lads. He was hit in the shins by a stick, and he cried out. History doesn't record what he said, but it was probably something like - "Oh Damn." Or perhaps something much worse.

Someone at the game shouted out "He Speaks", which in the language of the region is pronounced "Loughra". This is, actually, how Loughra acquired his name. History does not tell us what Loughra's name was before he got hit with a hurling stick. Perhaps he was not only speechless, he was nameless.

Loughra became a tall, strong and handsome young man., but with one physical deformity. He had huge, elephant-sized ears. Loughra hid his enormous ears by growing his hair long and combing his long hair over his elephant ears.

Once each year, Loughra needed a haircut. The barber, of course, soon discovered the elephant ears hidden beneath the long hair. As soon as the barber finished trimming Loughra's hair, Loughra killed the barber. This way, no one would know about his enormous ears.

Loughra's remedy was somewhat drastic, to be sure. He should have been able to get by with his barber knowing about the deformity. Or perhaps required an oath of secrecy. Loughra, it is certain, did not want to take any chances.

It didn't take too many years before the barbers of Brittany realized that cutting Loughra's hair was a fatal endeavor. Whoever cut his hair was never seen alive again. No one wanted the job thereafter.

So they conducted an annual lottery among the barbers. It was a lottery no one wanted to win. Whoever was selected by the lottery had to cut Loughra's hair, which was the last haircut the winning barber ever gave. Many barbers in Brittany sought other professions. It was about this time that the annals of

Ireland reported that a great many of the barbers of Ireland came from Brittany. This may or may not be a coincidence.

The handsome Loughra, with hair covering his enormous ears, had an eye for the young ladies of Brittany. Moriath was by far the prettiest of them all. She was beautiful, with mysterious eyes and long flowing hair. Loughra was one of the many young men who had eyes for Moriath.

Her father was among the most powerful nobles in Brittany. Neither he nor Moriath's mother believed that any man was good enough to marry their daughter. Moriath's mother was especially overprotective. Every night she slept with one eye open, so that she could always keep at least one eye on her daughter and on any amorous young man.

To woo Moriath, Loughra enlisted the help of his friend, a harper. There are those in the Celtic world who love harp music and it is beautiful to be sure. But for most people, listening to a harper guarantees slumber. It is difficult indeed to listen to harp music and stay awake.

The harper snuck up to the hallway of Moriath's home, outside the room of Moriath's mother. He played his harp -- and he played it well. He played a melodic tune, May Morning Dew, one of the most beautiful tunes ever played. Before long, Moriath's mother fell asleep. She could no longer leave her one eye open.

Loughra went into Moriath's room. And they did whatever it is that young people do whenever they are alone. Whatever it was they were doing, they did it all night.

When Moriath's mother woke up, she realized that she had been asleep with both eyes closed. She rushed to Moriath's room and discovered her in bed with Loughra. Mom was livid. But she was too late to do anything about whatever it was that Loughra and Moriath did all night.

There was only one way for her to make her daughter virtuous, and that was to allow her to marry Loughra. Thus the two were soon wed.

As a husband, and soon to be father, Loughra now had to find a job. He joined the army of the king of the Franks.

The Franks were Germanic tribes who lived along the Rhine River. Some moved west and called their new land France. Loughra gained fame as defender of the Frank king and rose through the ranks. He was a brave warrior and made many friends and allies.

After decades in France, Loughra decided to return to Ireland. This was not so much to avenge the murder of his father and his grandfather. But even after three decades, he still had the aftertaste from the mouse.

He brought with him an army of Franks and the Celts of Brittany and landed on the southern Irish shore. Loughra's mother, his wife and child, and his harper went with him too. Once in Ireland he was joined by enemies of Cova, for Cova was still king and had many, many enemies.

Loughra's army moved north and came to one of Cova's strongly garrisoned castles. The castle was quite formidable.

It was surrounded by a deep moat stocked with agitated seabass. Its walls were high. There were small slits in the castle walls for the archers, who could fire arrows on attackers and stay protected from return fire.

Loughra attacked the castle head on. Unfortunately, the attack failed miserably. Many men died from the archers' arrows before they could get close to the castle. Those few who made it to the moat discovered it too deep to traverse. Or perhaps the seabass too aggressive, or the castle walls too high. Loughra ordered a second direct attack which likewise failed.

Loughra called upon his harper to do his magic. He ordered his men to move as close to the castle as they could, without being in range of Cova's archers. He had them lie on the ground and cover their ears. Loughra did the same, although he needed help covering his ears, since, as you may recall, he had huge ears.

The harper then walked around the castle, playing his harp. The harper circled the castle three times. Soon all of the warriors inside the castle were asleep.

Loughra and his men then attacked - waiting for the harper to stop playing - and easily overtook the sleeping garrison. All inside were killed.

When news reached Cova, he thought it wise to make peace. He sent a messenger to Loughra. Loughra told the messenger to have Cova meet him at a neutral castle and the two would negotiate the peace terms there.

Loughra arrived at the meeting place first. His men set small fires throughout the castle. They made certain that there was plenty of kindling and combustibles everywhere. And finally, they placed huge bellows outside of the castle and hid them from plain view.

Cova arrived at the castle later, but he sensed a trap. Being somewhat sly, he said he would go into the castle for the meeting, but only if Loughra's mother went in first. He figured there could be no trap if he was accompanied by Loughra's mother.

Loughra's mother agreed, and entered the castle first. Cova followed. Once both were in, Loughra's men chained the doors shut. The men outside fanned the fires with the bellows. Soon the entire castle was in flames.

Cova was roasted alive. As was Loughra's mother.

Those outside heard her utter her last words: "I am happy to be roasted for the sake of my son."

With the roasting of Cova, Loughra assumed the throne of Leinster which once belonged to his grandfather, Leary.

You may have wondered. What would become of a boy forced to eat his father's and his grandfather's heart, as well as an entire mouse, a boy exiled from Ireland, a mute child who learned to speak after being hit by a hurling stick, a young man who stole the virtue of a maiden from Brittany, a friend of a magic harper, a soldier in the army of the Franks, a man who roasted his mother, a man with elephant ears, and a man who annually killed a barber?

And now you know the true story. He became the King of Leinster.

Potscript

This is my combination of several old Irish legends, in much abbreviated form. Like most of these legends, they are a millennium or so sold, told and retold by seanchaí for hundreds of years before being written down.

They were first written down in the 8th Century, mostly by Irish monks, sometimes in old Gaelic and sometimes in Latin. They were later transcribed into old English and later into more modern Irish or English.

While a good seanchaí could hold his audience spellbound for hours, it is sometimes difficult to plough through old written versions of these stories. When done, though, one reaches an "Aha" moment when it is discovered that buried beneath the archaic language is a wonderful story. My task, with this story and in many others I tell orally, is to retell the story in 21st Century vernacular – so that a modern audience will have the same joy attained by audiences a few thousand years ago.

About the Artist

Rob Wilkinson is an illustrator, storyteller and teacher from Whitley Bay on the northeast coast of England. He dabbles in cartoons, whimsy and occasionally dinosaurs. While teaching High School Science, and working for YMCA Camp Hayo-Went-Ha in Michigan, he has used his creative talents to enthuse and delight children and adults alike.

In 2012, Rob gained a distinction from London Art College in 'Illustrating Children's books', and has gone on to work on countless T-shirt designs, several yearbooks, charitable work and educational projects. This is his second published work, and he is working on several new projects, some of which involve dinosaurs.

Rob lives in an old terraced house, a few short strides from the North Sea, with his family, and two eccentric cats. His long association with the author is based on many shared moments of joy looking out upon Torch Lake in beautiful Northern Michigan.

He is on Facebook at @robwilkoart (Rob Wilkinson Art), and can be contacted via that page or at rwrobwilko@gmail.com.

About the Author

David McDonnell is an American author and story teller, with a passion for Irish and Irish-American history and folklore. He's traveled throughout the U.S. and Ireland sharing his love of history and his stories. His stories include factual and historical accounts, old Irish tales, Celtic legends, and plain old yarns.

ClanDonnell: A Storied History of Ireland, David's first book, won three national literary awards and received universally positive book reviews. *ClanDonnell* is a collection of true stories of an Irish clan which tell the history of Ireland in an entertaining, easy-to-read fashion. The tone is that of an oral history. The human stories, numerous illustrations, and humor bring the history of Ireland to life for the non-historian reader.

David spent most of his life in and around Detroit and received his bachelor's and doctorate degrees from the University of Michigan in Ann Arbor. He now lives in northern Michigan and enjoys the sunset over Lake Michigan almost every night.

More information is at www.clandonnell.net and David may be reached at clandonnell@gmail.com.